www.kindermusik.com

Written by Lissa Rovetch.
Illustrations by Holly Berry.
Book Design by Kym Abrams Design.

ISBN 1-58987-008-5

Published in 2003 by Kindermusik International, Inc.

Do-Re-Me & You! is a trademark of Kindermusik International, Inc.

Printed in China
First printing, July 2003

Frog Went A-Dancing

by Lissa Rovetch

illustrated by Holly Berry

"Hello, Elephant," says Little Frog. "I'm looking for a dancing song. Can you help me?"

"Oh yes," says Elephant. "I have the perfect dancing song!"

Singing, swinging,
Low and high.
Singing, swinging,
Trunk to the sky!

"That's the perfect dancing song for a
big elephant like you," says Little Frog.
"But not for a little frog like me."
So Little Frog goes to see Pig.

"Hello, Pig," says Little Frog. "I'm looking for a dancing song. Can you help me?"

"Oh yes," says Pig. "I have the perfect dancing song!"

Oink, snort, squeal!

Roll on the ground.

Oink, snort, squeal!

Spin yourself around.

"That's the perfect dancing song for a
rolling-around pig like you," says Little Frog.
"But not for a little frog like me."
So Little Frog goes to see Monkey.

"Hello, Monkey," says Little Frog. "I'm looking for a dancing song. Can you help me?"
"Oh yes," says Monkey. "I have the perfect dancing song!"

Giggle and jump!
Swing on a vine.
Giggle and jump!
Bananas taste fine.

"That's the perfect dancing song for a jumping-around monkey like you," says Little Frog. "But not for a little frog like me." So Little Frog goes to see his friend Otter.

"Hello, Otter," says Little Frog. "I'm looking for a dancing song. Can you help me?"

"Oh yes," says Otter. "I have the perfect dancing song!"

Splish and splash!
Shake your wet coat.
Splish and splash!
Sing while you float.

"That's the perfect dancing song for a splishy-splashy otter like you," says Little Frog. "But not for a little frog like me." So Little Frog goes to see one last friend.

"Hello, Bear," says Little Frog. "I'm looking for a dancing song. Can you help me?"

"Oh yes," says Bear. "I have the perfect dancing song!"

Growl and climb!
Tumble and fall.
Growl and climb!
Roll like a ball.

"That's the perfect dancing song for a growly climbing bear like you," says Little Frog. "But not for a little frog like me."

Little Frog hops slowly back home to his lily pad.
"Why are you looking so sad?" asks Mama Frog.
"I give up," says Little Frog. "I can't find the right
dancing song anywhere."

"Don't worry, Little Frog," says Mama Frog.
"I have the perfect dancing song for you!"

Hop a little, Swim a little,

Catch a juicy bug!

Ribbit to your partner,

And end with a hug!

"Yippee! That's the perfect dancing song for a big frog like you," says Little Frog. "And it's the perfect dancing song for a little frog like me, too! Thank you, Mama."

"You are welcome," says Mama Frog.
"Would you like to dance?"

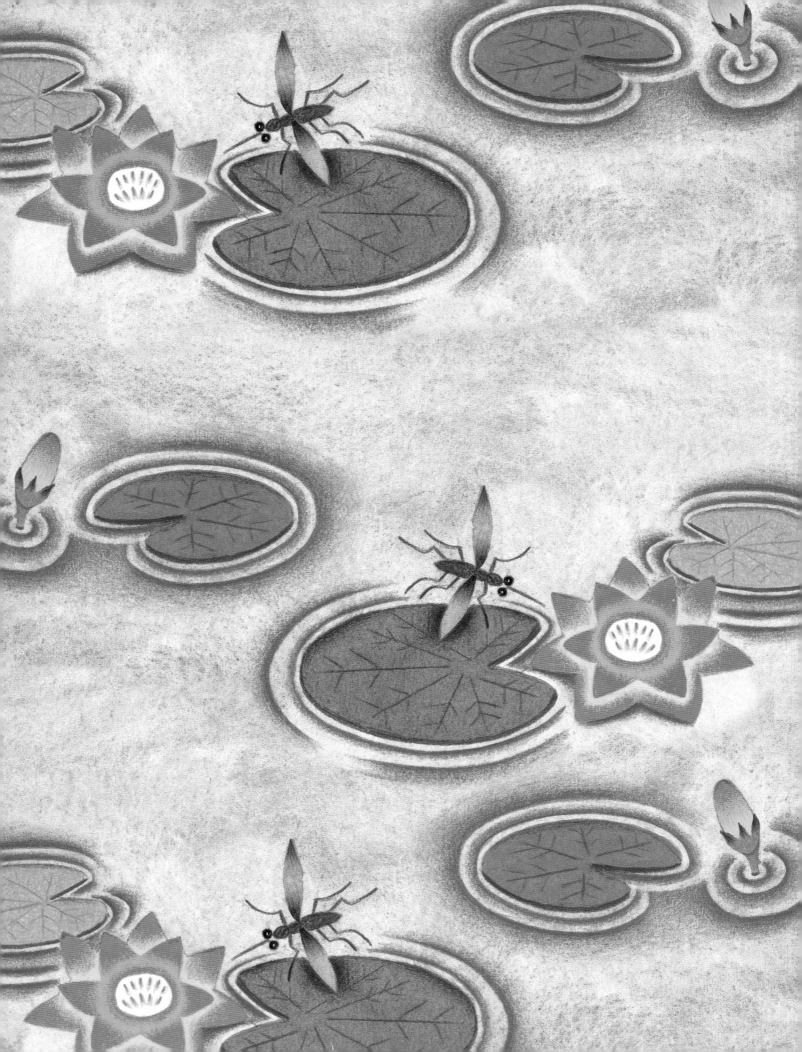